W9-BAK-804

DATE DUE			

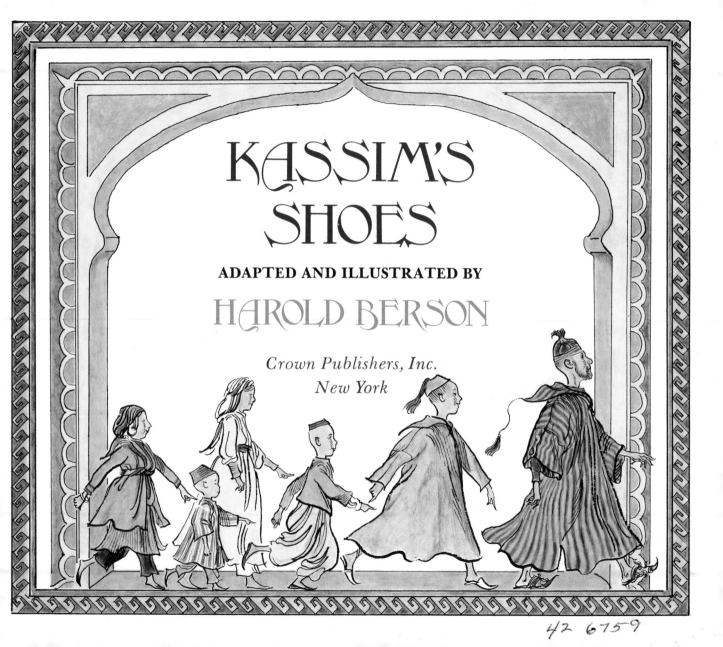

KASSIM'S SHOES

ADAPTED AND ILLUSTRATED BY

HAROLD BERSON

Crown Publishers, Inc.
New York

The text of this book is set in 14 point Baskerville. The illustrations are pen and ink drawings
with pencil shaded overlays prepared by the artist and printed in three colors.

Library of Congress Cataloging in Publication Data
Berson, Harold
  Kassim's shoes.
  Summary: Kassim succumbs to pressure to abandon
his old shoes but has trouble discarding them.
  [1. Folklore—Near East.   2. Shoes and boots—
Fiction]   I. Title.
PZ8.1.B419Kas3   [398.2] [E]   77-4688
ISBN 0-517-53063-5

10·25·78 BTSB 5.98

Also by Harold Berson

The Rats Who Lived in the Delicatessen

I'm Bored, Ma!

A Moose Is Not a Mouse

The Boy, the Baker, the Miller and More

Henry Possum

Balarin's Goat

How the Devil Gets His Due

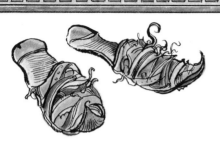

Kassim loved his old, patched-up, nailed-together shoes. They kept his feet dry when the streets were wet from rain. They kept his feet cool when the streets were hot from the noonday sun. They had been everywhere with Kassim, and he could not imagine owning a finer pair of shoes.

But his neighbors did not agree.

"How can you wear such ugly shoes?" cried Hassan the baker. "You are a disgrace to us all," mumbled Omar the melon vendor. "A shame," hissed Abdul the fig merchant.

"You have feet like a camel and walk like a donkey," shouted the children when Kassim passed.

One day Kassim's neighbors brought him a new pair of shoes. "They are fine shoes indeed," said Kassim. But to himself he thought, "Oh my, the leather is stiff, they are tight in the back and loose in the front." Tears came to Kassim's eyes. He knew he would miss his comfortable old shoes.

"Kassim is crying because he is so happy," said Omar the melon vendor, and everyone smiled with pleasure.

After they had left, Kassim could not decide what to do. "I know myself," he thought. "If I keep my old pair, I shall wear them instead of these new shoes. And then my neighbors will be angry all over again." Before he could change his mind, Kassim flung his old shoes out the window and into the river below.

The next day when the fishermen pulled in their net, they found a pair of old patched-up shoes mixed in with the fish. "Kassim's shoes!" cried Sadik the fisherman.

"Who else would wear such shapeless monsters?" said another.

The angry fishermen took the shoes to Kassim. "Throw these someplace besides the river," they shouted, and they left.

"So, my shoes are back again," sighed Kassim. Reluctantly he built a fire and laid the shoes in the flames. But the shoes were so water-soaked they only sputtered and smoked.

So Kassim put the shoes on his window ledge to dry. A neighbor's dog started to play with them, but the shoes fell from his mouth and landed on Fatima, the vegetable merchant's wife. "Ay-y-y," cried the startled woman, dropping all of her vegetables.

Kassim ran outside. "I'm sorry," he cried.
Fatima flung the shoes through Kassim's open
window. "What a nitwit you are!" she shouted.

That night Kassim tossed and turned in his sleep, wondering how to get rid of his old patched-up shoes. Suddenly he smiled. He jumped out of bed, picked up the shoes, and ran to the marketplace. Kassim climbed to the top of the tallest palm tree and stuffed his shoes among the clusters of dates. "There, my darlings," said Kassim, "you can stay forever, watching over the market during the day and enjoying the cool breezes at night."

In the morning the marketplace started to fill up.

There was Fatima with her vegetables,
Sadik with his fish, the basket weaver,
the spice merchant, the sweet seller,

Hassan the baker, Abdul the fig merchant,
and the poultry vendor.

Underneath the palm tree stood Omar
and his little donkey loaded down
with melons.

The morning wind blew in from the desert. It rocked the palm tree back and forth, rustling the leaves and shaking the clumps of dates. Suddenly Kassim's shoes fell right onto the back of Omar's dozing donkey.

The donkey kicked in every direction. Melons flew
through the air. Baskets toppled over.

Pastries fell to the ground.
Chickens flapped and squawked.

Vegetables and bits of pottery were
scattered everywhere.

Fatima was angry, Sadik was confused, and everyone was amazed. As they began to put the market back in order, Omar held up a pair of old patched-up shoes. "Can these be the guilty rascals?" he asked.

"Those are Kassim's shoes," said Sadik.
"I found them in my fishnet."
"Those are the shoes that fell on my head," said Fatima.
"What are they doing here?" asked Abdul.

A little boy who had been watching everything said,
"Perhaps the best place for Kassim's shoes is on his feet."
"I agree," said Hassan.

So Kassim's neighbors picked up the shoes and took them to Kassim.

Kassim put his new shoes in the closet, and he put
his old, patched-up, nailed-together shoes on his feet.

"Right where they have always belonged," he said.

That afternoon Kassim walked happily through town, and no one made fun of him.